Orchard Books, 95 Madison Avenue, New York, NY 10016

Manufactured in Belgium   Book design by Mina Greenstein
The text of this book is set in 14.5 ITC Slimbach Medium.
The illustrations are acrylic reproduced in full color.
1 3 5 7 9 10 8 6 4 2

Library of Congress Cataloging-in-Publication Data
French, Vivian.
Oliver's fruit salad / by Vivian French ; illustrated by Alison Bartlett.
p.   cm.
Summary: Although he loves to help Grandpa pick fresh fruit, Oliver will not eat
any until one day Mom prepares something very special in a big glass bowl.
ISBN 0-531-30087-0 (alk. paper)
[1. Fruit—Fiction. 2. Grandfathers—Fiction.]   I. Bartlett, Alison, ill.   II. Title.
PZ7.F889170j 1998   [E]—dc21 97-32704

Oliver's Fruit Salad

by Vivian French

illustrated by Alison Bartlett

ORCHARD BOOKS • NEW YORK

Oliver was eating his breakfast. He looked at his cereal and put down his spoon.
"When I was staying with Grandpa," he said, "I helped him pick crunchy red apples every morning."
"How lovely," said Mom.

When Mom made herself a cup of coffee, Oliver shook his head
at his glass of grape juice.
"At Grandpa's house, I saw *real* grapes. Gran let me
pick them. She made grape jelly."
"Goodness me," said Mom.

At lunchtime, Oliver's mother looked in the cupboard.
"Shall we have canned pears?" she asked.
Oliver sniffed.
"Grandpa *grows* pears," he said. "He doesn't eat pears out of cans.
He grows pears on trees."
"Lucky Grandpa," said Mom.

After lunch, Mom got their jackets.
"Let's go shopping," she said.
"Grandpa doesn't go shopping," said Oliver. "He grows *everything* in his garden."
"Hurry up," said Mom. "Put your jacket on."
"All right," sighed Oliver.

In the supermarket, Mom went to look at the jams.
Oliver told her about Grandpa's *wonderful* cherries
and strawberries and plums.
"Oliver," said Mom, "look over there."
"Why?" asked Oliver.

"Look!" said Mom.
Oliver looked. He saw apples and grapes and pears.
He saw cherries and strawberries and plums.
"Hmm," said Oliver. "I still think Grandpa's fruit is better."
"What about bananas and coconuts?" said Mom.
"Grandpa could grow them if he wanted to," Oliver said firmly.

Mom pulled up a shopping cart and filled it with fruit.
"I've never seen one of those in Grandpa's garden," Oliver said,
pointing at a pineapple.
"We'll buy a little one," Mom said, and she did.

Oliver helped Mom carry all the bags home.
They piled up the fruit on the kitchen table.
"Now," said Mom. "You can eat an apple. Or a pear.
Or a plum. It's not in a jar or a can. It's all fresh,
so help yourself."

Oliver shook his head.
"No, thank you," he said. "I just *helped* Grandpa.
I didn't *eat* any of the fruit. I don't *like* fruit."
Mom stared. "Oh, *Oliver!*"

The doorbell rang. Oliver rushed to open the door.
It was Gran and Grandpa.
"Hello!" said Oliver. "Come and see what we've got!"

Gran and Grandpa looked at all the fruit.
"FRUIT SALAD!" said Grandpa.
"What's that?" asked Oliver.
"Something very special," said Gran.
"We'll make it together."

Gran, Oliver, Mom, and Grandpa chopped up the fruit.
When it was all in a big glass bowl, Oliver smiled.
"It looks very pretty," he said.

Mom put out three bowls.
"Where's mine?" asked Oliver.
"You don't like fruit," said Mom.

"I like fruit salad," said Oliver, and he had three helpings.
"YUMMY!" he said. He licked his spoon thoughtfully.
"But I bet if it was all out of Grandpa's garden it would be even YUMMIER!"
And even Mom laughed.